This book
belongs to:
_____

Francis-the
Firehouse
Mouse

d.g.stern

NEPTUNE PRESS

NEPTUNE PRESS

WWW.NEPTUNEPRESS.ORG

Publisher's Cataloging-In-Publication Data
(Prepared by The Donohue Group, Inc.)

Names: Stern, D. G.
Title: Francis - the Firehouse Mouse / D.G. Stern.
Other Titles: Francis the Firehouse Mouse
Description: [Orlando, Florida] : Neptune Press, [2018] | Interest age level: 006-012. | Summary: Francis the Firehouse Mouse describes what it's like to work in a firehouse, to rescue people and pets from fires, and to teach fire safety.
Identifiers: ISBN 9780990610397
Subjects: LCSH: Mice--Juvenile fiction. | Fire fighters--Juvenile fiction. | Fire prevention--Juvenile fiction. | Mice--Fiction. | Fire fighters--Fiction. | Fire prevention--Fiction.
Classification: LCC PZ7.S74 Fr 2018 | DDC [Fic]--dc23

A hero is somebody who voluntarily walks into the unknown.

— *Tom Hanks—*

Hi!

I would like to introduce myself to you. My name is Francis. As you can see, I am a mouse. But I am not an ordinary mouse.

From the time I was very young, I was bigger than all the other mice, and I always wanted to be a firefighter.

Being a firefighter is a
very rewarding job.
You get to help put
out lots of different
kinds of fires and
sometimes save people and
even animals.

A firefighter has to be very strong. Every day you may have to climb a tall ladder or pull a heavy hose or go into a burning building.

As a firefighter, I get to sleep upstairs in the fire station above the fire trucks so that I will always be ready to help.

When the fire alarm rings in the station, we slide down the pole to get to our equipment and then climb into the fire trucks.

Sometimes we are called to a house fire. Not only do we have to put out the flames, we have to check to see if any people or animals are still inside.

Not long ago, we had to rescue a woman from a burning building. There was lots of smoke and some firefighters had to wear special masks.

When we get back to the station after a fire, each firefighter has to help clean up all of the equipment, including the trucks.

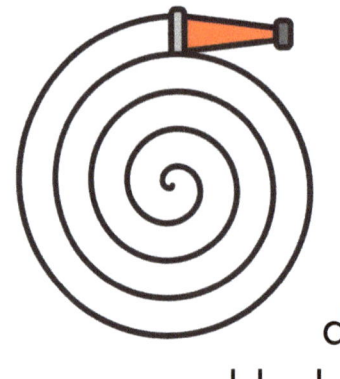

I have the best job cleaning up Sparky, our firehouse dog. Sometimes he gets so dirty that he looks all black instead of a spotted Dalmatian.

There have been a lot of car
fires recently. They can be very
dangerous because of all the gas.
 Occasionally people
in the burning car have
to be pulled out.

When it's hot, brush fires are very common. Sometimes the fires start because of lightning, but sometimes because people are careless or reckless. Don't ever play with fire!

A small brush fire can
easily become a
huge forest fire,
especially when there
is no rain and high wind.

People, animals, parks and
woodlands all suffer. Homes
are destroyed, wildlife
is endangered and the
environment is threatened.

A huge forest fire can become so big and dangerous that there is very little a firefighter can do.

We must be very careful to prevent forest fires.

Sometimes we work on water to save people. Flooding caused by heavy rain or hurricanes require us to go out in little boats and try to help.

Not only do people need to be rescued, but animals also need a helping hand—even getting a cat off a roof.

Firefighters are my best friends. We work  together as a team in order to do what we do best—keeping our community safe.

First responders; firefighters,
police, EMTs and emergency
room doctors and nurses
are always ready to
help—where ever and
whenever.

911

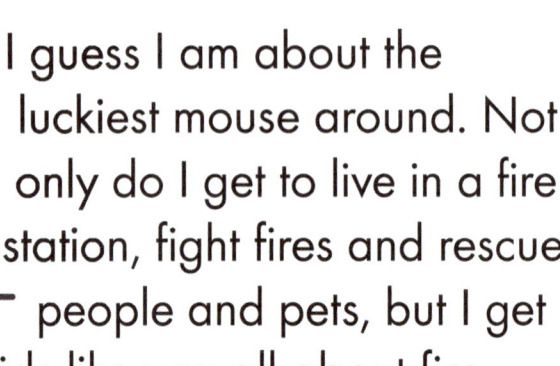 I guess I am about the luckiest mouse around. Not only do I get to live in a fire station, fight fires and rescue people and pets, but I get to teach kids like you all about fire safety.

Firefighters visit schools and hopefully you will visit us at your local fire station.

And always remember:

SAFETY FIRST.

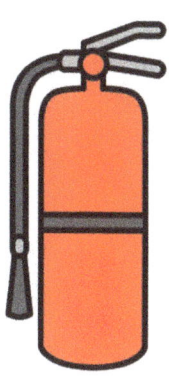

I hope to share more adventures
with you soon.

www.ingramcontent.com/pod-product-compliance
Lightning Source LLC
Chambersburg PA
CBHW051650120626
46551CB00015B/2291